Illustrated by Carlos and Jonathan Franco

A Note to the Parents

This book has taken me a lifetime to create, because I had to experience being a kid as an introvert, experience growing up as an introvert, experience being an introverted father as well as being a father to an introvert, and experience becoming a successful professional as an introvert.

Growing up I felt less than as an introvert. I marveled at how easily extroverts made friends, built networks, and worked around others. It was not until 2009 when I came to see my introversion as a positive of who I am as a son, husband, father, and professional. I came to understand the benefits of being me and I learned how to flex my style into extroversion in order to grow. Being an introvert is not bad or good. Being an introvert comes with strengths and opportunities. As parents, we want to help our kids tap into their strengths in order to excel, become the adults they want to be and take on the challenges they will be faced with throughout their lives.

This book is based on my lessons learned through my journey. Through reflection, I have come to formalize a model that I have used numerous times to help other introverts flex into an extroverted style. I do not have all the answers, but what I do have is firsthand experience as an introvert, one who has found great success being able to flex into an extroverted style. Implement the model so your children can find strength and confidence quicker than I did and please provide me with feedback so I can continue to support the introvert ninjas out in the world.

If you would like to learn more please contact me at Eric@iofranco.com.

A Note to Any Introvert Reading This

This book is for you. This book will help you uncover your strengths and learn to tap into those strengths to accomplish your greatest goals and aspirations. This book will help you to appreciate who you are more and more. Growth is not easy, but it is worth it. You are capable of so much. Being an introvert is a great thing. History is filled with successful introverts like:

- *Dr. Seuss*
- *Albert Einstein*
- *Mahatma Gandhi*
- *Abraham Lincoln*
- *Rosa Parks*
- *J.K. Rowling*
- *Michael Jordan*
- *Elon Musk*
- *Mark Zuckerberg*
- *and so many more*

No reason your name cannot get added to this list. You are not alone in this journey. Like me, you have others to lean on and learn from. Look for small growth daily and never be afraid to be uncomfortable to meet your potential.

It was a normal day in a town just like yours...

The Kids should be back soon from their first day at school, *said dad as he looked at his watch.*

Just then the door flew open, and their daughter came running in, **School was amazing! I talked to sooooo many new friends.**

That's great sweetie. Wash up and you can tell mom and I all about it.

Just then, dad saw his son walk in the door dragging his backpack and fighting back the tears.

How was your first day son? *asked dad, knowing the answer.*
It was awful! No one talked to me. I had to eat lunch alone, *said his son, Johnny.*
What happened? *asked dad.* No one talked to me, *said Johnny.*
There were so many kids at recess, so I just played by myself. I was a superhero saving the world, but when I went back to class everyone had made some friends except me.
Dad could see Johnny was sad and that made Dad sad too.
Dad thought for a few minutes and said, Son, I think you're an introvert.

OH No! Am I going to need a shot? *cried Johnny*
Ha, Ha, Ha, *no shots needed, said Dad.*
An introvert means you like being alone or playing alone sometimes because it helps you feel better. Your sister is more of an extrovert, which means she likes to be around a lot of people to feel better.

Does that mean she is better than me? *Johnny asked his dad*
No, being an extrovert or introvert is not good or bad. It is just one of many things that makes us who we are, and we are all uniquely great.
Let me tell you a story of a great superhero named the Introvert Ninja, *said Dad*
Wow, yes please, *said Johnny.*

It all started 10 years ago when a man was working on a project to protect the world, but there were so many villains trying to stop him.
The man knew he needed to help, but he was afraid to talk to other people because he was an introvert.
Just like me! *exclaimed Johnny*
Exactly, *said Dad*
What did he do dad?

This man wanted to be great, and he wanted to stop the villains, so he decided he was going to act like an extrovert..., sometimes.
It was at this time he decided to become the Introvert Ninja.
Whoa, that's so cool, *said Johnny.*

There was only one problem, he didn't know how to do it, *said Dad.*
So, what did he do dad?

First thing he did was honor who he was. He had to understand everything great about himself. One by one he listed everything he was great at. He wrote down

- ☐ smart,
- ☐ fast,
- ☐ great hair,
- ☐ kind heart,
- ☐ funny, and
- ☐ many, many other things.

At the end he had this really long list of things, but he was not done. Being a superhero is about getting better, so he listed three things he wanted to do better. He wrote down talk to other superheroes, talk in front of a room full of heroes, and talk about all the great things he can do, *said Dad.*

He was grateful for who he was, but he wanted to be more.

So, he was happy, but not done? *questioned Johnny.*

Exactly!

We should do the same thing, *said Dad.*

I want you to grab a toy, say something you like about yourself and place it in that corner.

Ok, *said Johnny.*

Johnny thought and exclaimed, **my strengths are:**
- **I'm fast.**
- **I'm great at my racecar video game.**
- **I'm smart.**
- **I have a great family.**
- **I make great toast.**

- **I'm good at soccer.**
- **I'm good at basketball.**

Now grab another toy and say one thing you wish you were better at and place it in that corner, *said Dad.*

Well... I want to talk to kids I don't know, and I want to know what to say.
Look at the room, son. Look at how many great things you listed versus the two things you want to get better at doing.

Seems like being an introvert is **awesome!** *Said Johnny.*
Being you is awesome, *said Dad smiling.*

HONOR TEMPLATE

Things I like about me

1. _____

2. _____

3. _____

4. _____

5. _____

6. _____

7. _____

8. _____

9. _____

10. _____

Things I want to be better at

1. _____

2. _____

3. _____

What about the Introvert Ninja, what did he do next, dad?

He made that list of the things he liked about himself, but really, that was a list of all his superpowers.

Whoa, *said Johnny.*

Next, he had to figure out how to power up, just like those superheroes do in your video games, *said Dad.*

How did he recharge? *asked Johnny*

He found that working out or sitting alone reenergized his superpowers.

Wait! I feel better when I sit by myself too, *said Johnny.*

Exactly, and you can still do that to recharge your superpowers, *said Dad.*

Let's think of a few more ways you can recharge your superpowers, son.

Johnny named the following ways he can recharge:

- **I like to be alone too.**
- **I like playing video games.**

- **I like to shoot hoops.**
- **Oh, I like to color too.**

Why does the Introvert Ninja need to recharge, dad?

Well doing things that are hard or uncomfortable can drain your powers quicker. It's like when you use a special power in one of your video games. The superhero can only do it for a little while because it uses a lot of their power.

Oh, I understand now, *said Johnny.*

Does that mean I'll use my superpowers quicker too, since talking to other kids scares me?

Yes, growth can be a little scary, *dad said,* but we all have the ability inside to do these things. This is also why the Introvert Ninja needed to know how to repower, just like you need to know.

ENERGY TEMPLATE

What brings me energy

1. _____

2. _____

3. _____

4. _____

5. _____

6. _____

7. _____

8. _____

9. _____

10. _____

Examples

Coloring	Singing
Reading	Playing a video game
Playing a sport	Talking to a friend
Playing with toys	Watching tv or a movie
Building something	Dancing
Helping mom or dad	Drawing

Did the Introvert Ninja talk to other superheroes? *asked Johnny.*

Yes, he did. He put a plan in place to talk to one new superhero a week, but he made sure he could sit alone afterwards, because he needed to recharge.

What about you son? What do you want to try first?

I want to talk to some kids at school, but that sounds scary.

I know it does, but that's why we will use your superpowers and setup a plan, *said Dad.*

How do I do that dad?

Well why don't you try to talk to one kid at recess, then when you go back to class you can sit alone and color or read to energize, *said Dad.*

I can try that, but how do I go talk to a kid I don't know? *asked Johnny.*
Let's use your list of superpowers. Ask someone to play soccer or basketball with you, *said Dad.*

Let's wash up for dinner.
What about the rest of the story, dad?
Let's have you practice tomorrow, and I'll tell you the rest of the story tomorrow after school, *said Dad.*
Ok, dad.
The next morning, dad went to go check on Johnny getting ready for school.

How do I know if I can do it? *asked Johnny.*
Let me show you something, *says Dad.*
Dad stands next to his son as he looks in the mirror.
What do you see? *asks Dad.*
I see me, *said Johnny.*

Look closer.
You know your superpowers.
You know what recharges them.
Dad pointed to the mirror and said, **look at the kid that is smart, makes great toast, loves to play soccer, and has so many other great superpowers.**

Johnny sees himself as the Introvert Ninja and smiles with confidence.
I'm ready dad, *Johnny said, with a huge smile.*
Awesome, use those superpowers.

Later that day the door flies open with Johnny running in yelling I did it! I did it!
I played soccer at recess with Aaron.
That's great son, *said Dad, with huge smile.*
I am the INTROVERT NINJA!, *yelled Johnny.*
Can you tell me the rest of the story, *asked Johnny?* Yes, let's see where did we
leave off?

The Introvert Ninja just finished talking to other superheroes, *said Johnny.*
Oh yes, *said Dad.*

In the Introvert Ninja's mind, he just finished battling his #1 villain because talking to
other superheroes was so hard. So, he went back to his hideout to think about what
he could have done to be better. That's what superheroes do, *said Dad.*
What do you mean? Didn't he do it? *asked Johnny*
Yes, he did, but he knew he was nervous, and he could do it better the next time, so he
wanted to review what happened and see what he could improve. The Introvert Ninja
made some small mistakes, like calling one of the superheroes by the wrong name. It
was a little embarrassing, but the other superhero just laughed, *said Dad.*

I was nervous too, and I do have to do it again tomorrow so maybe I should review too, *said Johnny.* **What did he do?**
He made a list all the things that went well and he listed two things that could have gone better.

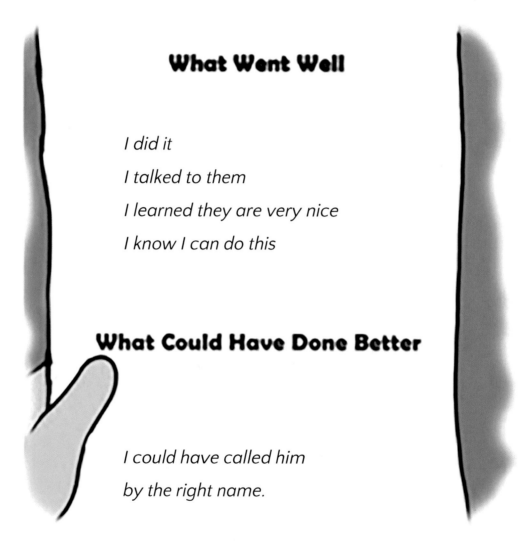

What Went Well

I did it

I talked to them

I learned they are very nice

I know I can do this

What Could Have Done Better

I could have called him

by the right name.

Let's do the same thing with you. What went well and what do you wish went better? *asked Dad.*

REVIEW TEMPLATE

Things that went well

1. I did it

2. _____

3. _____

4. _____

5. _____

6. _____

7. _____

8. _____

9. _____

10. _____

Two things I wish went better

1. _____

2. _____

What do you think you can do tomorrow? *asked Dad.*

Tomorrow I'm going to bring my coloring book. That way, I can color to energize after recess, and I can show my expert coloring skills. What about the Introvert Ninja dad? What happened next? *asked Johnny?*

He continued to do these things to get better. He has beat a lot of villains and most people now do not think he is an introvert, *said Dad.*

If I keep doing these things, will I get better too? *asked Johnny.*

Yes, you will. The Introvert Ninja knew he had to get better each day. It's a journey, *said Dad.*

Thanks for the story dad. It helped me. I love you! I love you too, son.

Johnny feels better, *said dad.*
That's great, *said mom.*

Did he ask who the Introvert Ninja was? *said mom.*
Nope.

The End

Introvert H.E.A.R. Model

This book is based on the Introvert HEAR Model. It is used in my coaching sessions with introverts to help them flex into extroverted styles. If you would like more information on the model or know someone who could benefit from it, please contact me.

HONOR: Acknowledge and Celebrate Who You Are

ENERGY: Embrace What Energizes You, and Understand What Drains You

ACT: Take Action

REVIEW: What Worked and What Can Be Improved

info@introvertninja.com
Introvertninja.com

Thank You

This book could not have been written without the help and inspiration of so many. First and foremost, to my wife for being the first to see this introvert's potential and inspiring me to be more and do more. Next to my kids for bringing life to me daily. Thank you, Jonathan, Carlos, Ilizabeth and Victor. I hope this inspires you to stretch past your comfort. Thank you to all those that supported me in my journey and those that sought out my coaching.

A special thanks to my two illustrators (Jonathan and Carlos). I had a blast working on this book with you. This will be a memory I will cherish throughout my life. Each of you grew through this process and I look forward to your continued growth.

Made in the USA
Middletown, DE
25 June 2021